BULLIES
Change of Hearts

Chapter One

Ding dong!

"Kier, the girls are here!" yelled Kiersten's mom, Mrs. Jeri Shorter, or Ms. J, as everyone called her.

"You girls ready for the big game?" she asked as she opened the door to let the girls into the house. Each one carried a gift and overnight bag.

"Yes!" replied Abbie, Kelly, and Bella at the same time.

"Is Kiersten ready for the game?" asked Abbie as she and the other girls sat down at the breakfast bar that was covered with sweets and appetizers.

Abbie was a great athlete, tall and strong, and always wore her blond hair in a ponytail. Some kids called her a tomboy, which made her upset. She was book smart but sometimes lacked common sense.

Bella loved soccer but was a total girly-girl with her curly red hair and spotless peaches and cream complexion. She didn't like to get dirty or to break a nail. She cared about her appearance more than the average person and was always applying makeup for pale skin.

Kelly loved technology and math. With her black braided hair, bronzed skin, and tall stature, she looked like a model. Out of the three girls, Kelly was the closest to Kiersten, and they live just two houses apart. Bella and Abbie live in the neighborhood as well but on a different street.

"If the birthday girl ever comes downstairs, you can ask her yourself," Ms. J said jokingly.

"Kiersten is so lucky to have a caterer as a mom. And not just any caterer, but the best!" said Bella. "That chicken Alfredo you made for our class was so good!"

"Thanks, Bells," replied Ms. J She gave every-one a one-syllable nickname; she called Abbie, Abs and Kelly, Kels.

"Hold on! I'll be down there in a sec! I'm getting dressed!" Kiersten yelled down the stairs.

Ms. J went to the staircase and yelled, "Hurry up; everyone is waiting on you!"

"I'm sorry she's taking forever," Ms. J told the girls. "Help yourself to some food. If you wait on Kier, you may have to play on an empty stomach."

Kelly and Abbie rejected the offer because they wanted to be nice and wait on Kiersten. "No, thank you, we'll wait for Kiersten," they replied.

"Ha ha ha! Not me," said Bella as she made her way to the buffet. "More for me!"

"We'll go get Kiersten," said Kelly.

"Go ahead. I'll watch over the food," Bella said as she waved to them.

Kelly and Abbie started up the stairs. "Wait!" shouted Kelly as she quickly stopped on the stairs. "Let's go see what Ms. J got Kiersten for her birthday," she whispered.

The girls quickly went back down the stairs and into the kitchen.

"Ms. J, what did you get Kiersten for her birthday?" asked Kelly.

Ms. J smiled and looked at the excitement on the girls' faces. "It's a surprise."

"We won't tell," said Abbie.

"We promise," added Bella.

"You promise, Kels?" asked Ms. J.

"We promise!" The girls vowed.

"Okay, I got her..." Ms. J said and hesitated.

"What?" the girls said in unison.

"A dog." Ms. J whispered.

"OMG! I love dogs!" Abbie said with a big smile.

"We know!" responded Kelly and Bella.

"What kind?" asked Abbie.

Before Ms. J could answer, Kiersten walked into the kitchen. "It's about time, slowpoke!" said Ms. J.

"Yeah, we thought you were gonna miss the game and your birthday," added Bella.

"No way am I gonna miss today! We're gonna win the championship, and then we're going to party!" Kiersten said as she danced around. All the girls started dancing and cheering.

"Kiersten, where's your sister?" asked her mom.

"I thought she was already down here. I'll go get her."

Kiersten ran upstairs and stopped in Josie's doorway. Josie was video chatting on her cell phone with one of her friends, asking her to ask her mom if she could spend the night over at her house. Josie added, "I know Kiersten is not gonna want me around with all her friends tonight." Kiersten stood behind her, listening to the conversation.

"Yeah, who wants their little sister around?" added Josie's friend. Kiersten and Josie were three years apart in age. Josie was in the 5th grade, and Kiersten was in the 8th.

"Um, I do," interrupted Kiersten. Kiersten took Josie's phone and told her friend that Josie would call her back. She sat next to Josie on her bed and put her arm around Josie's shoulder.

"What do we always say?"

"Sisters by blood, best friends by choice," they said in unison.

"But your friends probably wouldn't want me around, especially now that you're 13," added Josie.

"Now, Madam President," said Kiersten because Josie was voted class president, "my friends love you, and they know you're my best friend. If they don't want my BFFL around, then they don't want me around."

Josie smiled. "Seriously?"

"Yep, and if you want, you can invite a couple of your friends. Make sure you invite Annita. That girl is crazy!"

Josie smiled again. "My BFF is the best."

"I know," Kiersten said, laughing.

"But what about Justin? Is he gonna be here?" Justin was their 6-year-old brother.

"He's going to be here for a little while, and then he's going to spend the night with one of his friends. Tyrone, I think," replied Kiersten. "Tonight is girls' night. He understands. But, I do hate that we'll miss his game."

"I know. I wonder how many touchdowns he's gonna score."

"Let me think...Probably three!"

All of a sudden, Kiersten was attacked by her friends. "Get off of me!" Kiersten said, giggling.

"Well, come on!" said Kelly. "It's game time."

"Is our number-one fan coming to the game?" Bella asked Josie.

"You know I have to go cheer for my BFF!" replied Josie as she smiled at Kiersten.

"No, Kiersten is my best friend," said Kelly as she hit Josie with a pillow.

"No, she's my BFF!" said Bella as she hit Kelly with a pillow. Next thing you know, they were in a full-blown pillow fight!

"Girls!" Ms. J shouted. Scared that they were in trouble, they stopped dead in their tracks because they should have been on their way to the game by now. "I can't believe you all are having a pillow fight without me!" She grabbed a pillow from Kiersten and joined in the pillow fight.

***

Kiersten and her friends piled into the back of Mrs. J's SUV to go to their soccer game. Josie sat upfront.

"Josie," Kiersten called. "Why are you sitting up there?"

"I'm keeping Mommy company," she replied. She *really* sat upfront because she didn't think Kiersten wanted her in the back with her friends.

"I think Mom will be okay if you came back here. Right, Mom?" asked Kiersten.

"I don't know; I need my little navigator." She looked in the rearview mirror and winked at Kiersten. "I think I'll be okay," she said to Josie. "Go ahead." Josie leaped up with a big smile and headed to the back with Kiersten and her friends. Before Ms. J could back out of the driveway, her phone rang...

"Hey, Honey," said Ms. J. It was her husband, Gerald Shorter.

"You going to be okay dealing with Coach McLendon today?" asked her husband.

"I'm sure after the talk you two had; he won't be starting trouble today."

"Okay, Justin and I should be there by halftime."

"Okay, Honey, see you soon."

"Tell the girls I said good luck," he said as he hung up the phone.

"Ms. J," said Abbie, "I have a question. Well, not a question but an observation. No, actually, it's a question."

Ms. J, laughing as she always did with Abbie's silliness, replied: "What's your question/observation/question?"

"I bet you never realized this, but did you know your first name, Jeri, is the nickname for Mr. G's first name, Gerald?"

The girls looked at Abbie to see if she was kidding with the question.

"No," laughed Mrs. J "I haven't realized that in the 19 years we've been together."

"Really?" replied Abbie.

"She's kidding, Abbie," said Kelly. Everyone laughed.

"No, like, for real Kiersten! Like, your mom and dad are both named Jeri Shorter!"

"Mom, I have a question," said Kiersten. "I mean, it's definitely an important question."

"What is your important question?" replied her mom.

"What did you and Daddy get me for my birthday?"

"What do you think we got you for your birthday?"

"I don't know. Maybe a gift card or a tablet?" replied Kiersten. "I know it's not what I really want—what I've been wanting for years..."

"What have you been wanting?" asked Kelly.

"A dog," replied Kiersten. "But someone doesn't think that I'm responsible enough to have one," she said as she looked at her mom. Kelly, Bella, and Abbie bit their tongues and said nothing about the dog.

"I know what she got you!" Kelly teased.

"You do?" Kiersten said shockingly.

"Yeah, we do too!" added Abbie and Bella.

"So do I!" said Josie, laughing.

"You have to tell me!" Kiersten said, dying to know.

"We're not telling you," Abbie said with a big smile. Kiersten begged all the way to the soccer game, but they still didn't tell her.

Chapter Two

When they arrived, Kiersten, Abbie, Bella, and Kelly ran to the soccer field to join their team-mates.

"Hey, Kiersten!" shouted Stats, one of their teammates. Stats's name was actually Evelyn. Her nickname was Stats because she knew stats on just about everything.

"Hey, Stats!" Kiersten shouted back as she ran toward her.

"Happy birthday!" she said as she hugged Kiersten.

"Happy birthday," mocked her teammate Charlie. "Who cares about your birthday? It's game time," she said as she walked away.

"Well, looks like Charlie's in a good mood," Bella said jokingly.

"I'm not going to let her spoil my mood," said Kiersten. "You know why?"

"Because it's your birthday?" Abbie responded with a smile.

"Yep!" She started singing as she danced toward the field. "It's my birthday! It's my birthday! It's my birthday!" The girls approached the field, laughing and dancing excitedly about the game and the party later.

"Can't you losers focus on the game?" shouted Charlie.

Charlie's dad, who was also the coach, added, "Yeah, girls, if you can't get your head in the game, then you need to leave my field." He turned and looked directly at Kiersten and said, "Now run and tell yo' momma I said that!"

Without the coach knowing, Ms. J had walked up behind him. "I've heard all I need to hear," said Ms. J. "Coach McLendon, can I talk to you over here?"

"I don't know if you're aware, Jeri, but we're getting ready to play a game, and I ain't got time to talk to you," said Coach McLendon as he walked away.

Ms. J caught up with him and said, "I have told you if you can't respect these girls, then they're not going to play—especially my child!"

"Your child sucks anyway, so you can take your child and get off my field!"

"Girls!" called Ms. J. "Get your things. We're leaving."

The four girls gathered their things and began walking away. Other parents saw them leaving and called out for Ms. J to wait. Ms. J was so upset that she didn't stop until she got to her SUV. When the parents caught up with her, they asked what happened.

"McLendon has crossed the line this time. I will not have him continue to insult and disrespect these girls."

"Please stay! We truly need the girls," said one of the parents.

"You want me to allow my child to continue to be bullied by him? That's out of the question. No game is worth these girls' self-esteem being lowered."

"He's a great coach," said another parent.

"Girls, get in the car," said Ms. J. "I know he is a good soccer coach, and that's why I wanted Kiersten to play on his team, but while everyone was telling me how good of a coach he was, they forgot to mention that he was a bully."

Patricia McLendon, Coach McLendon's wife, approached the group of parents. "Jeri," she said, "are you really going to leave?"

"Absolutely," responded Ms. J. "If you want to show your kids that bullying is wrong, you would be leaving too. Seriously, Patricia, I don't know how you put up with him! He's a bully and abusive."

The remaining girls, with the exception of Charlie, went to their parents and said they didn't want to play. Charlie began walking toward her mother.

"Charlie, get your butt back here now!" shouted Coach McLendon as Charlie continued toward her mother.

"Mom," Charlie said urgently, "I don't want to play either. Dad is—"

Before she could finish, Coach McLendon interrupted, "Didn't I tell you to refer to me as Coach McLendon? Now get your butt back over here!" he shouted.

"Mom, please," cried Charlie.

"Dan," said Mrs. McLendon, "she doesn't want to play."

"Shut up, Pat! Don't you dare contradict me! Now both of you get back over here," he said as he pointed to the field.

Mrs. McLendon looked at the other parents ashamed as they looked back at her in shock. She grabbed Charlie by the arm. "Come on, sweetie," she said as they walked back to the field.

Coach McLendon continued angrily, "Now, as for the rest of you, if you want to teach your kids to be quitters, then leave. If you want them to be winners, let them stay and play!"

"We're not teaching our kids to be quitters! We're teaching them to stand up to bullies," yelled Mrs. J. All of the parents and kids got in their cars and left.

On the ride back, the girls were quiet. They had never seen Ms. J get so upset. "Ms. J?" said Abbie finally.

"Yes, Abs?"

"Thank you so much for standing up for us. My mom would have never done that."

"Yeah," agreed the other girls. "You are the bomb!"

"Thank you, sweetie, but I'm sure if your mom had been there, she would have done the same thing. I'm sorry you girls had to be a part of that." She turned on the radio. "Kier, your song's on!" She turned the music up louder and bobbed her head to the beat. The girls loosened up a little because they saw that Ms. J was in a better mood. The girls began singing and moving to the beat.

"Kiersten, your mom is so cool!" said Kelly.

"I know, right?"

As Ms. J pulled into her garage, her phone rang. It was her husband. "Hi, honey."

"Justin and I rushed to catch some of Kiersten's game and found out it was forfeited. What happened?" Mr. Shorter asked.

Ms. J, knowing how protective Mr. G was of Kiersten, didn't really want to tell him what happened. "Everything's okay, and we're just getting home. I need to call Annette and let her know we're home so she can bring that package she's been holding for us."

"So you're not going to tell me what happened?"

"Okay, I've gotta go, but do you mind picking up some ice on the way home? I love you, Honey! Bye-bye!" she said hurriedly.

"Real smooth, Mom," said Kiersten as she got out the car.

Ms. J hung up and called Annette, their 19-year-old neighbor. "Hi, Annette! We're home." She turned to her daughter. "Kiersten, will you meet Annette halfway so you can get that package from her?"

"Is it for me?" asked Kiersten.

"It's for the party."

"Will you just go?" shouted Kelly.

"Okay," replied Kiersten. "Y'all not coming with me?"

"Hello!" said Abbie. "Our hands are full!" she replied as she held up her gear bag in her hands.

As Kiersten turned to walk down the street, she saw Annette coming. "Oh well, I'm too late. Here's Annette now," said Kiersten.

Annette walked up with a fluffy white dog on a leash. "Hi, Annette," said Kiersten as she walked toward her. "Wow, did you get a new dog?" she asked as she knelt to pet him. "He's beautiful!" The girls and Ms. J tried to contain their excitement. "What's his name?" asked Kiersten.

"Read his tag!" said Annette. Kiersten read the tag:

To: Kiersten

Love,

Mom & Dad

It took a second for Kiersten to understand what she had just read. "Really?" she shouted. "He's mine?" she said as she embraced the dog.

"Yes!" shouted her friends and Josie with big smiles.

"You guys knew about this?" asked Kiersten.

"Yeah!" replied her friends, excitedly.

"You too, Josie?"

"Yep!" she replied with a smile.

Kiersten picked up the dog and hugged her mom. "Thank you, Mommy! This is the best present ever!"

"You're welcome, baby."

"What are you going to name it?" asked Bella.

Without hesitation, Kiersten responded, "JJ."

"JJ?" questioned Josie.

"Yeah, after my two favorite people."

"Um, my name starts with a K," said Kelly.

"Yeah, I know," said Kiersten, laughing.

"Ohhh," it finally dawned on Josie who Kiersten was talking about. "You're so sweet," said Josie.

"Yea, that's pretty cool," said Kelly.

"Wait, who are J and B?" asked Bella.

Everybody laughed. "Josie and Justin!" they said in unison.

"Ohhhh right," said Bella.

"Just remember to scoop his poop," said Abbie.

Chapter Three

Back at Kiersten's house, the girls were getting ready for the party in Kiersten's bedroom.

"This party is gonna be lit!" said Kelly.

"I know, right?" agreed Bella.

"Is Jacob coming?" asked Abbie, trying to hide her excitement.

"I knew you liked him," said Kiersten with a smirk.

"I just asked if he is coming. That doesn't mean I like him!"

"Um, yes it does. It means you like him and you want him to be your bae and you want to take long walks on the beach!" said Kelly, laughing.

"Yeah, and you want to put his name with a lock by it on Instagram," added Kiersten.

"Yeah, and you want him so you can say hey," added Abbie.

"Huh?" everyone teased as they threw pillows at Abbie.

"Speaking of Instagram, let's see if anyone is talking about your party," said Bella.

"Let's take a pic and post," said Abbie as she reached for her phone.

"Noooo, I look like a hot mess! I need a shower!" said Bella as she tried to tame her hair with her hands.

"Girl, ain't nobody gonna be able to tell you funky from a picture," teased Kelly as she pinched her nose. "Come on; let's take a pre-getting ready pic!"

The girls posed for the picture, and Kiersten posted it on Instagram with the caption "Getting ready to get ready for my birthday party! #seeyasoon #finally13."

"You should have put #doublestufforeo," said Abbie. "You know, since me and Bella were in the middle," she joked.

"I have a question," said Bella. "Well, not a question but an observation," she joked, mocking

Abbie from earlier. "Kiersten, why is it that you're having a pool party, but you're not gonna swim?"

"Yeah, if I had an indoor pool, I'd be swimming every day," added Bella.

"Well, I can't," said Kelly, laughing. "My hair will be even nappier than it is now."

"That's exactly why I'm not going to swim. I just got my hair fixed. I ain't tryin to mess it up," said Kiersten.

"Well, if Jacob is swimming, I'm swimming," said Abbie, laughing.

"I'm not," added Bella. "I'm going to be in the DJ booth, mixing it up!"

"You mean you gonna be at the DJ booth watching your bae mix it up," said Kelly.

"I swear, you and Latrell are my relationship goals," added Abbie.

"Nah, Kiersten and Zack are my relationship goals," said Bella.

"Zack and I are not a couple," said Kiersten, "...yet."

"Let's see all the hearts he puts under your post," said Bella.

The girls checked their phones and saw that Charlie had commented under the picture, "Wow, 4 of the ugliest people in the same room." Kelly saw the comment and went ballistic.

"I'm so tired of her and her mouth! She always has a negative comment," said Kelly.

"Yeah, like she's some cyberbully," added Abbie.

I'm glad you didn't invite her!" said Kelly.

"I did invite her," replied Kiersten. "She didn't respond; so, I guess she's not coming."

"Good," said Abbie.

"Come on, Charlie's okay," said Kiersten. "I believe her dad is the issue. We were all cool until her dad became our coach."

Kiersten commented under Charlie's post, "LOL! You know we're beautiful. Are you coming to the party?" Instead of posting a reply on Instagram, Charlie texted Kiersten.

"You're so fake. How you gonna be on Instagram asking me if I'm coming to your party when you didn't invite me?"

Kiersten replied, "I did invite you. Check your direct messages. That's how I invited everybody. Anyway, I hope you come."

***

Charlie threw her phone on her bed without reading Kiersten's response and stomped downstairs teary-eyed. Charlie's mom heard her stomping down the stairs.

"What's wrong?"

"Stupid Kiersten is posting pictures about her stupid party that she didn't invite me to," pouted Charlie.

"I'm sorry you didn't get invited, sweetie. There'll be other parties."

Charlie's dad stood in the doorway looking at Mrs. McLendon consoling Charlie. "You both are pathetic!" shouted Coach McLendon. "Why are you babying her? So what if the little monkey didn't invite you to her party?"

"Dan!" shouted her mom. "That language is not necessary," she added.

"You don't tell me how to talk! Now stop baby-ing her and go make me some dinner!"

"Dan, I'm talking to Charlie. I'll finish cooking in a minute."

He walked over to Mrs. McLendon and grabbed her by the arm.

"Ouch, you're hurting me, Dan!" said Mrs. McLendon, as he pulled her away from Charlie.

"Dad, stop!" yelled Charlie. "You're so mean to everybody. She probably didn't invite me because of you!"

He stopped pulling his wife for a second. "You think I care about how that little brat feels? I don't. And if you ever take that tone with me again, you won't ever go to any party. How did I end up with two weak kids and a pathetic wife?" Just then, his son DJ walked into the house. "Speak of the little weakling, and he appears," said his father.

DJ looked at his mom and sister and saw fear in their eyes. "Mom, what's wrong?" he asked.

"Pat, get in there and make my dinner," he shouted as he pushed her toward the kitchen.

"Dad, no!" shouted DJ.

"Dad, no!" mocked Coach. "Are you going to stop me? I can't believe how weak you are. You don't deserve to have my name. Here, I'll push her again," he said as he shoved his wife more forcefully. DJ stood in his spot with his fist clenched. "Do something!" taunted his dad.

"Dan, okay, I'm going to cook. Just calm down, both of you."

Charlie sat quietly, too scared to move or make a sound. Her dad walked over to DJ and stood eye to eye.

"You think you're man enough now to take me down?"

DJ stood, staring at his dad. His dad walked away and sat down. DJ continued to stand. "Go get me a beer," he told DJ.

"Get it yourself."

Charlie jumped up. "I'll get it!" She ran into the kitchen, grabbed a beer, and handed it to her father. He snatched the beer and stared at the can. Charlie turned to walk upstairs when, all of a sudden, she felt a thump on her head. Her dad had thrown the beer can at her.

"I told DJ to get me a beer, not you."

Charlie screamed in pain and ran upstairs. DJ charged his dad, and Mrs. McLendon ran into the room from the kitchen.

"DJ, no!" shouted his mom. Dan grabbed DJ and put him in a submission hold. "Let him go, Dan!" she said as she grabbed his arm. He pushed her away, and she hit the wall with a thud.

"No!" shouted DJ. He mustered the strength to free himself from his dad's hold and run over to help his mom up.

"Are you okay, Mom?" asked DJ.

"Yes, just go upstairs," replied his mom wearily.

"No, Mom, I'm tired of him bullying us around," DJ responded. His dad stood, staring.

"What do you think you're gonna do?" asked his dad. "You ain't gonna do anything because you're too weak. That's why your little girlfriend broke up with you. That's why you're a second-string quarterback."

"First of all, I stopped seeing her because I didn't want her around you; and I'm a sophomore on the varsity team; and yea, I'm the backup quarterback. But I'm not the weak one—you are!"

"Who do you think you are, talking to me that way?" He grabbed DJ by his hair and pushed him toward the floor. "Drop and give me 100 pushups!"

"No!" shouted DJ. His dad grabbed him and threw him on the floor, standing with his foot on his son's back.

"What are you going to do? Either hit me or give me my pushups!" shouted his dad.

"DJ, just do them," pleaded his mom.

"No! He calls me weak, but I'm not the weak one! He is!" he said, staring at his dad. "You're the one who thinks that bullying your wife and kids makes you a man. You think that by hurting the only people in the world who love you, that makes you strong? No, it doesn't. It makes you weak! You think by pushing Mom, kicking me, and hitting Charlie in the head makes you a man?"

"You did what?" his mom exclaimed.

"Yea, Mom, he hit Charlie in the head with a beer can."

"Dan, you've gone too far this time." Mrs. McLendon ran upstairs. "DJ, bring me some ice," she yelled as she made her way to the top of the stairs. When she arrived at Charlie's room, she found Charlie crying on her bed.

***

Back at Kiersten's house, the girls were reading all the comments under the picture on Kiersten's post.

"Man, everybody's gonna be here," said Abbie.

"Yeah, and it looks like everybody's glad that Charlie's not coming," added Kelly.

Kiersten looked in her closet, trying to decide what to wear. "Why do you say that?"

"Because of all the comments under the picture you posted."

Kiersten picked up her phone to see the comments. She began deleting the negative comments and then added her own, "Charlie is more than welcome to come to my party, and if anyone has a problem with that, then they can stay at home."

"Wow, Kiersten, I don't know how you can like her when she's so mean to you," said Kelly.

"Like I said, Kels, we were all friends until her father became our coach. I think he's making her be mean to us. I don't know why she changed, but I still consider her my friend, and I want her to come. I'll text her again to see if she's coming."

Hey, are you coming to my party?

"Come on, let's shower so we can get the party started," said Kiersten as she put her phone in her pocket.

"I call Kiersten's shower!" shouted Kelly.

"I got Josie's!" shouted Bella.

"I got Ms.—" started Abbie.

"Don't even think about it!" said Kiersten. "I have my parents' bathroom."

"Man, why do I always have to go downstairs?" asked Abbie.

"Kier, don't take forever like you always do when you use your parents' shower," said Bella.

"But it's so big and cozy with all the showerheads. Okay, I'll try to hurry," said Kiersten.

Downstairs, Ms. J and Josie were setting up for the party. The doorbell rang, and a smile crept across Ms. J's face. "I guess someone's early. Josie, will you get the door?"

Josie went to the door and opened it. Ms. J followed. Josie stood, shocked to see that it was Ms. J's pregnant twin sister Vivian along with her husband Fred from California standing in the doorway.

"Uncle Fred!" Josie shouted and leaped into her uncle's arms. She had not seen him in years because he was in the military. Ms. J hugged Aunt Viv and walked her inside.

"Kiersten is going to be so surprised and happy to see you, Aunt Viv," said Josie excitedly.

"I know! I Facetimed her this morning. She told me how badly she missed me and that she wished I was here to celebrate her 13th birthday with her. It was hard keeping it a secret," said Aunt Viv.

"It sure was," agreed Ms. J. "I wanted to tell you, Josie, but I know how close you and Kiersten are, and I knew you would have said something."

"Does Daddy know?" asked Josie.

"No way, he's worse than you trying to keep a secret! He's going to be so surprised to see you, Fred."

"I can't believe it's been four years since we've been here. Thankfully, we have all this modern technology like Facetime and Facebook to keep in touch," said Uncle Fred.

"But there's nothing like seeing you all in person," added Aunt Viv. "Where's the birthday girl?" she asked, looking intently around the room.

"She and her friends are upstairs getting dressed. I'll go get her," said Josie.

"Josie, don't spoil the surprise!" said her mom.

"I won't," smiled Josie as she ran upstairs.

Ms. J squeezed Fred's bicep and said, "Now let's put those muscles to work!" She walked them into a room with a swimming pool, big screen TV, and party decorations.

***

Josie went to Kiersten's room where Kelly, Abbie, and Bella were waiting on Kiersten to get out of the shower. "Kiersten!" Josie shouted with excitement.

"She's still in the shower," they all said.

"Y'all come downstairs! I want you to meet my aunt and uncle," whispered Josie. "Kiersten doesn't know they're here."

"Is this the famous Aunt Viv?" whispered Kelly.

"Yes."

The girls went downstairs. When they entered the pool room, they all hugged Aunt Viv.

"Let me see, I have Facetimed with all of you," Aunt Viv pointed. "Kelly, Abbie, and Bella," she said, and she was right. Uncle Fred entered the room, carrying some chairs.

"Uncle Fred!" they shouted and went to help him with the chairs. They all introduced themselves.

"Girls, go grab some trays and chips from the kitchen and put them on the table."

The girls entered the foyer with bags and bags of chips and some trays. Then they heard Kiersten fussing. "Why did y'all leave me like that?" she pouted.

"Well, you were taking forever, and the party ain't gonna set itself up! Now grab some of these bags and help us," said Kelly. Kiersten grabbed some bags of chips and followed them into the party room. Kiersten entered the room, still fussing about being left behind. She didn't see Aunt Viv because she was behind the other girls. The girls stepped aside, and Kiersten stopped in mid-sentence. She couldn't believe her eyes!

"Aunt Viv!" she yelled. She dropped the bags and ran to hug Aunt Viv. "OMG!" she said, "You're here!" Kiersten said, tearing up. "I thought you said you couldn't fly because you're pregnant?"

"I wanted to surprise you," said Aunt Viv as she wiped Kiersten's tears. "Did you *really* think I'd miss your 13th birthday?" Kiersten heard a deep voice clearing his throat; she turned around.

"Uncle Fred!" she leaped into his arms. "I thought you were in Afghanistan?" she cried.

"I got home two weeks ago, for good," he said, squeezing her in a tight bear hug.

"This is the best birthday ever! Josie, did you know they were coming?" asked Kiersten.

"No, Mommy didn't trust me. She thought I would've told you."

"Yeah, you probably would have," said Kiersten, laughing. "Does Daddy know?"

"You know your daddy can't keep secrets," replied Ms. J.

"He's going to be so surprised!" said Kiersten.

"He should be here any minute now."

"Whew, I need to go to the restroom," said Aunt Viv.

"Are you okay?" asked Kiersten.

"Yes. It's just that being pregnant, I have to use the restroom a lot," she sighed.

"I'm sure you're tired from that four-hour flight too," added Ms. J.

"I am a little tired. I'll take a little nap after Gerald gets here."

"I'll call to see where they are. Josie, walk Aunt Viv to the restroom," said Ms. J as she took her cell phone out of her pocket to call her husband. Then, she heard the front door being unlocked.

"That must be them," said Kiersten. "Mom, let me see your phone, so I can record daddy when he sees Uncle Fred!"

"Fred, get behind the door!" said Ms. J in a hushed voice.

Her dad entered the room. "Where's the birthday girl?" he asked. Mr. Shorter was a bit of a neat freak and frowned at the bags of chips on the floor. "Why are there chips on the floor?" he asked as he surveyed the room.

"I put them there," said Uncle Fred with a huge grin as he stepped out from behind the door.

Mr. Shorter turned and saw Uncle Fred. "Aw, man!" he said. "When you did you get here?" They embraced and stepped back to do their special handshake.

"You're holding up pretty good, old man," said Uncle Fred.

"I see being in the service, you finally got some muscles on those bones," responded Gerald. Justin stood, looking at Uncle Fred curiously. He was 2 years old the last time he saw him, so he didn't recognize his uncle.

Uncle Fred grabbed Justin. "What's up, man? I know you don't remember me, but I'm your Uncle Fred! We'll have plenty of time to get to know each other because guess what?"

"What?" replied Justin.

"We're moving back to Atlanta!"

"Really?" said Mr. G.

"Yeah, man, I'm out for good now."

"This is cause for a celebration!"

Kiersten stopped recording and said, "But we already are celebrating!"

"Yes, we are," agreed her dad. Kiersten put her mom's phone on the table and received a big hug from her dad. "I can't believe I have a teen-ager. And not just any teenager, but a beautiful, caring, intelligent, perfect teenager," he said as he hugged Kiersten. "Viv couldn't make the trip?" asked Mr. G.

"She's in the restroom," replied Kiersten.

"There was no way she was going to let me come without her," added Uncle Fred. "You'd think Kiersten was her daughter," he added.

"Yes, I love the bond they have," said Ms. J. "When Viv would babysit Kiersten, she would pretend she was me, and she got away with it. So, she's like a second mom to her."

Aunt Viv waddled back into the room. "Justin!" she shouted. He ran to Aunt Viv and hugged her.

"Hi, Aunt Viv," said Justin. "Now I see why you didn't answer my Facetime call this morning!"

"Yes, after I talked to Kiersten, I had to jump on the plane. How did you do at your game?" asked Aunt Viv.

"I scored three touchdowns," said Justin. Kiersten and Josie smiled at each other, remembering Kiersten's three-touchdown prediction earlier.

"Wow," said Uncle Fred, "you must have skills like your Uncle Fred!"

"Three touchdowns," said Aunt Viv. "That's cause for a celebration!"

"But we're already celebrating!" said Kiersten, laughing.

"You have some amazing kids," said Aunt Viv. "A football star, a class president, and the most well-rounded 13-year-old I know."

"Thank you," replied Ms. J., "I'm sure that little one you're carrying is going to be amazing if she is anything like her mom."

"You mean if he is anything like his dad!" corrected Uncle Fred.

"Josie and I are going to marry brothers when we get older like you and Aunt Viv did," said Kiersten."

"You have years and years to think about marriage," said Ms. J.

"Yeah, years and years and years," added Mr. G.

"But yes, y'all did get lucky to find us," Uncle Fred joked.

Aunt Viv playfully elbowed Uncle Fred.

"I mean we were the ones who got lucky," said Uncle Fred with a sheepish grin.

"You got that right," agreed Mr. G as he kissed Ms. J on the cheek.

"Ew," said Justin.

"Trust me, you won't be thinking ew in about 5 years," said Mr. G.

"Yeah, lil bro, the girls are gonna be after you, and you're gonna change your mind about kissing," teased Kiersten.

"Whoa, wait; are you thinking about kissing someone?" asked Mr. G.

"Zack," said Kelly under her breath.

"No, sir, I'm not thinking about kissing any-body, but why is it okay for Justin when he's 11 but not for me at 13?" asked Kiersten.

"Because he's the man," said Uncle Fred.

"Right," agreed Mr. G. "Man, I can't believe you're here," said Mr. G. "We need to take man's trip to the store and get some premium spirits," he added.

"Did you remember the ice?" asked Ms. J.

"Let's go get some premium spirits and some ice," said Mr. G. Everyone laughed.

"Yes, all of us men," said Uncle Fred. "You ready, Justin?"

Justin smiled. "I can go?"

"Anybody who scores three touchdowns in one game is obviously a man," said Uncle Fred.

"Honey, will you bring me some of that Geor-gia peachy cream juice?" asked Aunt Viv. "You know, the one in the green and peach bottle."

The three guys looked at each other because they had no idea of the drink she wanted. "I love that drink," said Josie. "Daddy, will you bring me a bag of crunchy jalapeño and cheddar chips?" she added.

Mr. G. looked more confused. "Okay, let's take a 'three men and a special little girl' trip to the store."

"Yeah, I've heard about this custom purple Caddy truck you have. Hand over the keys!" said Uncle Fred.

"You know I had to represent that purple and gold," replied Mr. G. "I'm glad you're here, but you ain't driving the purple heart!" he continued, clutching his prized keys a little closer.

"While you guys go back and forth, I'm going to take a little nap," said Aunt Viv. "Girls, can I borrow Kiersten for a couple of minutes?"

The guys and Josie started toward the door. "Don't forget the ice," reminded Ms. J

"Wait, let's take a picture," requested Kiersten.

"I'll take it," said Kelly.

"Hold on, I got to get the newest member of the family," said Kiersten. She ran and got JJ.

They took a variety of pictures, some with just family, some with Kiersten's family and friends.

Chapter Four

Aunt Viv was relaxing on Kiersten's bed with Kiersten sitting next to her, enjoying their time together.

"Thanks for letting me crash on your bed," said Aunt Viv.

"Anything for my favorite Auntie," replied Kiersten.

"I'm your only Aunt!" she said as she gave a quick chuckle.

"But if I had a hundred of them, I'm pretty sure you'd be my favorite," replied Kiersten with a loving smile.

"So, is Zack coming to the party?" asked Aunt Viv.

"Yes," Kiersten replied blushing.

"Has he asked you out yet?"

"He did, but I told him that he had to talk to my dad."

"What did he say to that?"

"He said he was going to talk to him tonight."

"Oh, so he has good taste plus he's brave!" said Aunt Viv, laughing.

"Yes, and he's cute, smart, and athletic." She blushed an even deeper shade of red.

***

At Charlie's house, Charlie lay face down on her bed as her mom rubbed her head where the can had hit her. "Mom, I'm okay. I just want to be left alone," said Charlie.

"You sure?" asked her mom.

"Yeah," she replied quietly. Mrs. McLendon left the room. Charlie picked up her phone and read her messages from Kiersten. She checked her direct messages on Instagram and saw the invite that Kiersten had sent. She texted Kiersten.

"Hey, I just saw your invite. I would like to come if you still want me to come."

She ran downstairs where her parents were arguing. "Mom," she said with excitement, "Kiersten did invite me to her party, like 2 weeks ago! I just didn't see the invite. Can you walk me to her house?"

"Didn't I tell you that you weren't going over her house?" shouted her dad.

"Charlie, go upstairs. I'll be up there in a minute," said her mother.

As Charlie sat in her room, waiting for her mom, she received a reply from Kiersten.

"Of course, I want you to come. Let me know if you need us to meet you halfway."

"My dad is tripping. I don't think I'm going to be able to come," texted Charlie.

Kiersten replied, "You have to come! If you're not here in 15 minutes, my mom and I are coming to get you!"

***

"Aunt Viv, I'll let you rest. Thank you so much for coming," said Kiersten. "You really made my day. I have to go get Charlie with my mom."

"It was so hard keeping it a secret. I'm glad I could make it. And guess what? When we move back after having the baby, I'm going to work with your mom, and we're going to open an eatery!" said Aunt Viv.

"That's going to be awesome!"

"Well, come and get me when you get ready to cut the cake. This little one inside of me has a sweet tooth," said Aunt Viv, laughing and rubbing her round belly.

"Sure, blame the baby," Kiersten joked. "So are you *sure* you don't know if you're having a boy or girl?"

"I know, but Fred doesn't know I know."

"What is it? I promise I won't tell!"

"I can't tell you. Fred doesn't even know!"

"Okay, I understand," said Kiersten disappointedly. "Do you need anything before I go back downstairs?"

"No thanks, sweetie. I just need a little rest."

Kiersten covered Aunt Viv with a throw blanket and gave her a big hug. She turned to walk out of the room.

"Hey, Kiersten, I hope she's as wonderful as you are," said Aunt Viv with a sly smile.

"She?" replied Kiersten as she put her hands over her mouth, giddily.

"Yes, shhh!" replied Aunt Viv.

Kiersten motioned as if to zip her lips. She closed the door and went downstairs.

More guests had arrived, including Zack. "Let me take a picture of y'all," said Kelly. Zack and Kiersten posed for the picture.

"Here," said Kiersten, "take one with my phone." Kiersten gave Kelly her phone and posed for the picture.

"Kiersten," said her mom, "if you want to go get Charlie, then we need to go right now before everyone gets here." They hurried out of the house and started to Charlie's.

***

Back at the corner convenience store, Josie wanted to split up to start her shopping. "Daddy, may Justin and I go to the candy aisle?" asked Josie.

"Sure. Make sure you watch your brother and pick something out for your sister too."

As Josie and Justin made their way to the candy aisle, the man at the cash register stared at them. Justin picked up a bag of candy. "Do you think Kiersten would want these?" asked Justin, laughing.

Josie started laughing. "She absolutely hates that candy!"

"I know. We should get it just to be funny."

"Nah, we would be wasting money."

"What are you kids doing over there, stealing?" the cashier screamed.

Mr. G and Uncle Fred both turned to see the employee yelling at Josie and Justin. "Is he serious?" asked Uncle Fred, astonished at the situation.

"I know your type," said the clerk. "You come in here and steal! All of you people are bad."

"What d'ya mean by 'you people'?" shouted Uncle Fred as he walked toward the man standing behind the counter. The store employee took a step back.

"Bro, calm down," said Mr. G.

"No way; he's accusing my niece and nephew of stealing and talking about 'you people.' He doesn't mind taking us people's money!"

"What money? You always want something for free. You and your homie need to buy something or get out of the store!"

"Bruh, is he serious?" asked Uncle Fred, shocked at the clerk's hateful words.

"You send your kids to the front of the store so you can steal," said the clerk.

"Wait, are we stealing or are the kids?" asked Mr. G. sarcastically.

"You're all stealing!" He knocked on a window to get the attention of the policeman who was just outside.

"Josie and Justin, let's go," said their dad, frustrated with the situation.

"No, you're not going anywhere, you thief!" shouted the owner as he raised his finger in the air.

Just then, a White, middle-aged policeman entered the store. "What's the problem, Hasib?" the officer inquired as he popped peanuts in his mouth.

"Check them thug kids. They're stealing!" The employee cast a judgmental finger in their direction.

"Thugs?" shouted Mr. G as he walked toward the employee angrily.

The policeman, Pete Kilpatrick, stepped between them with his hand over his baton on his waist belt. "Boy, you need to calm down."

"Boy?" shouted Uncle Fred. "He's a grown man. Who the fu…" Uncle Fred caught himself from using bad language in front of his niece and nephew. "Who do you think you are, disrespecting my brother like that?"

"I'm talking to you, homeboy. Now, you gonna calm down and tell me which of these brats is the thief?" The officer practically spits the words out at the group.

"What! Neither one of my kids is a thief," shouted Mr. G. Josie, and Justin stood shocked and scared, unsure of what they should do.

"I don't get you people," said the officer. "You stand here with your fancy watches and nice shoes, and I saw you get out of that nice purple Cadillac, but you send your kids to steal."

"Man, let's get out of here before I end up in jail for hurting this man... I mean, boy I've got a pregnant wife I need to get to," said Uncle Fred.

Officer Kilpatrick took out his baton. "You address me as officer."

"I'm giving you the same respect you gave me. Address me as sir, and I'll address you as officer."

"Let's go," said Mr. G.

"I can't let you leave. Now, Hasib here seems to think that someone has been stealing. I'm going to have to check all of you," said the officer, matter-of-factly.

"You check the video and tell me what reason he has besides us being Black to want to check us," said Uncle Fred.

The officer put his baton back in its holder and began tossing more peanuts in his mouth as if to dare Uncle Fred and the group to ignore him and leave. He began to cough. The officer's face turned red as he coughed more forcefully. He grabbed at his throat, the coughs muffled by the peanut lodged in his throat. He was choking! Everyone stood frozen in shock, looking at the officer. "Do something, Daddy," said Justin. "Save him, Uncle Fred," cried Josie. Quickly, Uncle Fred grabbed the officer and gave him the Heimlich maneuver. The peanut popped out, and the officer bent over and put his hands on his knees. He was able to breathe. Officer Kilpatrick looked up at Uncle Fred, who had just saved his life, struggling to slow his breath. He said nothing.

"Let's go," said Mr. G. They began walking toward the door.

"Wait, you can't leave," said Hasib. "Officer, check them!"

"Shut up, Hasib," said Officer Kilpatrick, rubbing his sore throat.

"It's unbelievable that people still act that way. Prejudging people because of the color of their skin," said Uncle Fred as they got in the car.

"What's really weird is that Mr. Hasib's skin is darker than ours!" said Josie. They all laughed, which helped to lighten the situation.

"We won't be going back to that store. Let's not tell anyone what happened until tomorrow, okay?" said Mr. G.

"Okay," they all replied.

"Let's just go to the package store. I'm sure they have the drink Vivian wants," said Mr. G.

"Okay, because you know I can't return without it," said Uncle Fred.

"Daddy, don't forget that we have to get some ice," said Josie.

"Forget the ice?" said her father. "I hadn't forgotten. I'm the man!"

"You forgot, huh, bro?" asked Uncle Fred, laughing.

"Yeah, I did."

"Watch out!" shouted Uncle Fred as he saw a semi-truck running a red light.

The out of control semi-truck, running a red light, plowed into them, pushing the Caddy into a light pole on the corner. The sounds of screeching tires, metal against metal, and shattered glass were loud and terrifying, and after the dust began to settle, there was no movement or sound inside the mangled SUV.

Josie moved slowly. Bleeding and hurt, she struggled to reach her cell phone. In pain and crying, she dialed Kiersten's number. Kiersten didn't answer, so she left a message. "Kier," creaked Josie. "We've been in a bad car accident. Nobody is moving. I'm so scared. Kier, I love you. I love Mom, too. I'm glad you're my best friend."

***

Kiersten and her mom arrived at Charlie's house. They rang the doorbell. Charlie's mom answered the door. She looked disheveled as if she'd been crying.

"Hi, Pat," said Ms. J. "Are you okay?"

"Yes, I'm okay. What can I do for you?" asked Mrs. McLendon as she stood with the door barely open.

"We came for Charlie," said Kiersten. "I would like for her to come to my party."

"Sorry, we would have called when we were on the way, but we both left our phones," Mrs. J apologized.

"Charlie!" called her mom. Her dad stood behind the door. Charlie came running downstairs with her overnight bag in her hand.

"Bye, Mom!" she said as she quickly went out the door. They began to walk back to Kiersten's house.

"Man, you look like you're escaping," joked Kiersten.

"Well, actually I am," said Charlie. "My dad was really tripping. He didn't want me to come. I'm so glad you came to get me. I'm sorry for what I posted on Instagram today and for being mean. You're a good friend, and I miss hanging out with you."

"I've missed you too. But we're cool. I'm glad you're coming."

When they arrived back at the house, Ms. J noticed that Mr. G had not made it back from the store. "They must've gone to the store in Florida," joked Ms. J. "I'll call him when I get in the house."

They entered the pool room. No one was in the pool. There was no music playing. Kiersten spotted Kelly and Abbie. They had tears in their eyes, and everyone was staring at the TV.

"What's going on?" asked Kiersten. "We're supposed to be partying!"

"Has anyone seen my phone? I need to call Gerald to see what's taking them so long," said Ms. J.

No one said a word. Ms. J and Kiersten looked up at the TV. It was breaking news. The headline shouted with red letters on white, 4 Killed in an Accident with a Semi truck. Reporters were at the scene of the accident. Along with fire trucks, ambulances, police cars, you could see a mangled SUV. The SUV had the same unique purple color as Mr. G's.

"No!" screamed Kiersten. "No, no, no, no, no!"

Kelly, Abbie, Bella, and Zack rushed to Kiersten's side. Ms. J stood there in shock. All of a sudden, she fainted. Zack caught her before she hit the floor. He laid her down on the floor.

"Someone call 911!" he shouted.

"Here, put these pillows under her knees," said Charlie, who was out of breath from running to get the pillows. "You have to elevate her legs."

Kiersten dropped to her mother's side. "Mommy, no, I can't lose you too. Mommy!" she cried.

"I think she just fainted," said Zack as he brushed the hair from Ms. J's face. After several minutes, Ms. J opened her eyes to see Kiersten by her side, crying.

"Are you okay, Mommy?" cried Kiersten.

"What happened?"

"You fainted." They helped Ms. J to her feet. As she was getting up, Aunt Viv came into the room.

"Where's my cake?" she asked. She looked around the room and realized she was looking into the faces of sadness. Kelly turned off the TV before she had a chance to see the news.

They heard the doorbell, and Abbie and Bella ran to let in the paramedics. Along with the paramedics, there were police officers. Ms. J, now on her feet, told Aunt Viv to come into the living room so she could talk to her. Aunt Viv looked at Kiersten, who was crying hysterically.

"Kiersten, what's wrong?" she asked, suddenly unsure of whether or not she wanted to hear what Ms. J was going to tell her.

"Come on, Vivian. Let me talk to you."

The paramedic entered the room. "Is everyone okay in here?" He saw Ms. J trying to walk. She was still a little dizzy from fainting.

"Ma'am, are you okay?"

"I'm fine. I need to talk to my sister in here."

The paramedic assisted Ms. J and Aunt Viv into the living room. "Sit down," said Ms. J.

"Jeri, what's going on?" asked Aunt Viv.

Just then, a policeman came into the room. It was Officer Kilpatrick from the store. He was crying.

"Your husband saved my life," he said to Aunt Viv. "I was at the scene and when I realized who they were. I wanted to be the one to tell you—"

"Officer, please, let me talk to my sister," interrupted Ms. J.

"Tell me what?" Aunt Viv asked the officer, panic beginning to shake her voice.

"I'm sorry, but—" started the officer, but he was cut off again by Ms. J.

"Officer!" Ms. J said sternly. "Will you do me a favor and go ask the kids to call their parents to come get them?'

"Yes, ma'am," the officer said softly.

Chapter Five

Five months after the tragic accident, Mrs. J and Kiersten were still trying to deal with their loved ones being gone. Kiersten, who was once vibrant and outgoing, was now secluding herself in her bedroom, playing Josie's voicemail over and over, crying every time. Her eyes had become blood-shot from crying and not sleeping. She had lost weight from not eating.

"Kier," her mom said as she was coming down the hallway to her room. "Here, baby, I made your favorite chicken noodle soup and grill cheese, and I brought your friend with me." Just as she said that Kiersten's dog jumped on her bed. She smiled a little when she saw JJ.

"No thanks, Mom. I don't feel like eating."

"I know, Kier. I feel the same way, but we have to eat. We have to eat for each other."

"But Mom, I miss them so much." She began to replay the message. Her mom took her phone and placed it on the bed. Then she sat down with a sigh.

"Kier, I have to talk to you about something. I've been waiting and waiting, hoping to find a good time. But there's just no good time." Kiersten, hearing the seriousness of her mom's tone, sat up.

"Mom, what is it?"

Her mom took her hand, softly rubbing it, and began to cry.

"There's really no easy way to say this. You know how I told you I had breast cancer before you were born?"

"Yes, ma'am, but you beat it. I mean, it's gone, right?"

"Yes, but sometimes, chemotherapy can cause you to have leukemia, and that's what I have. I thought I was just feeling down because of the accident, but I realized that I'd been having shortness of breath, nosebleeds, and bruising, so I went in for testing.

"What does this mean? Do you have to go through chemo again?"

"Yes, baby. Actually, I start chemo on Monday. With the kind of leukemia I have, I'm going to need a bone marrow transplant. For the past 2 months, I've been on the list at Be The Match. Hopefully, they can find someone who matches me to donate bone marrow."

"You've known about this for two months?"

"Yes, baby. I really didn't want to add to what you're already dealing with."

"Knowing that you've been dealing with this by yourself makes me feel terrible."

"I don't want you to feel terrible. I just want you to be happy and get back to doing things you like to do like hanging with Abby, Kelly, and Bella and playing soccer. You know, Pat and Charlie have been here every day since the accident. Charlie and the girls really want to be here for you. You've got to get back to your life. I know it was tough the last few months of school and I'm grateful that they allowed you to finish the year from home, but after the summer, you have to get back in school. I may be a little too tired to help with your schoolwork. Wow, my baby's going to be in high school."

"Did you ask Aunt Viv if she could be a match? Or is she still not speaking to us?" asked Kiersten, ignoring what her mom had just said.

"Kier, like I said before, I don't think it's that she's not speaking to us, I just haven't been able to contact her. We both took time to grieve and, unfortunately, her phone was disconnected. Listening to the messages, she left me; she was upset that we didn't come out to California to support her when she had little Fredericka. I understand that, but I just couldn't pull myself together to go. I had just found out about my leukemia; I just couldn't go, and there was no way to tell Aunt Viv."

"It's never too late to go see them. If it means saving your life, let's go, like tomorrow," cried Kiersten.

"I've called her cell every day for the past month, hoping that she will have it turned back on. I'm worried about her. It's not about saving me. I just really miss my sister. I just can't get in touch with her."

"What about me? Can I be your donor?"

"No, baby, you're too young."

"I don't care. If I'm a match, I'm doing it." She started eating the soup. "I need to eat so I can be strong enough to donate. Those doctors won't deny me an opportunity to save my mom's life. And when you lose your hair from the chemo, I'm shaving my head too."

"You're so thoughtful. I love you so much, but you don't have to do that."

"I love you too, Mom. I want to do it. It's only hair."

"I'm glad to see you eating. But do you know what will really make me feel better?

"What, Mommy? You name it."

"If you call the girls and we have a girls' game night."

"Yes, ma'am. I'll call them."

"Thank you, baby. I'll see what snacks I can whip up for us."

"No, Mom. I'll make the snacks. You just get some rest."

"Now, Kier, you know I love cooking for you girls. I'll be okay. I want you to focus on being happy. Let's play Scattergories, so I can beat y'all like I always do."

"Yes, ma'am," Kiersten said softly.

"Come on, Kier, where's the smack talk? I'm going to be okay, but if I see you upset and worrying, it's going to make me stressed. So, I need you to be the Kiersten of old for me."

"I'll do my best, Mom. I promise."

"Thank you, baby, and I promise not to beat y'all too badly tonight."

"You mean you promise not to cheat," said Kiersten, laughing.

"I don't cheat."

"Yes, you do. The last time, you were sup-posed to name a president whose name started with M. You said, Mr. Jimmy Carter. Then you thought just because he's the only president from Georgia that we were going to let you slide. And when we didn't, you, all of a sudden, got an 'important' call and had to stop playing."

"I don't remember that," said Ms. J innocently. "Go ahead and call the girls. Ask Charlie and Kelly if their moms can come too."

***

That evening, as they sat around the large ta-ble in the living room playing Scattergories, everyone was racking their brains, naming things in the refrigerator that started with the letter I.

"For that, I have ice-cold milk," Ms. J said boastfully.

"Oh no, Ms. J is back to her cheating ways," Kelly said jokingly.

"What? That's a good one," smirked Ms. J. "Well, I have to get the cookies out the oven anyway, so just skip me this game."

Everybody laughed. "If she can't have her cheating way, she quits," said Kiersten.

Ms. J stood up and stumbled a little. Kiersten jumped up quickly to help her mom.

"Mom, are you okay?"

Everyone looked surprised that Kiersten jumped up like that just because Ms. J tripped.

"Mom, I'll get the cookies; you just keep cheating," said Kiersten.

Kiersten walked into the kitchen and began to cry. Kelly, worrying about Kiersten, followed her.

"Kiersten, what's wrong," Kelly asked as she hugged her.

Kiersten couldn't hold it back any longer. Her friend's hug was so comforting. She cried harder.

"My mom has cancer, and she needs someone to donate bone marrow."

"Oh no," said Kelly. "You guys have gone through so much. This can't be happening. I'm so sorry, Kier. Is there anything I can do?"

Kiersten cried harder and harder. Kelly tried to be strong for her friend but she couldn't hold back her own tears.

"We have to be strong for my mom. I don't know if she wanted me to tell anyone, so don't say anything when we go back in there."

"Okay," agreed Kelly through her tears.

They cleaned up their faces and took the cookies out. When they returned to the living room, Kelly tried her best not to make eye contact with Ms. J because she knew she wouldn't be able to control her tears. She thought of Ms. J as her second mother. Ms. J noticed Kelly trying not to look at her. Ms. J extended her arms to Kelly for her to come hug her. Kelly went over to Ms. J, now crying and hugged her.

"I'm sorry, Ms. J; I'm so sorry," said Kelly.

"It's okay, Kels. I'm going to be okay."

"What's going on?" asked Kelly's mom Belinda.

Belinda got up to comfort Kelly.

"Baby, what's wrong?" She looked at Kiersten, who was crying as well. "Kiersten, what happened in the kitchen?"

"I'm pretty sure Kiersten told her that I have cancer," said Ms. J.

"Oh no, Jeri," said Belinda. She embraced both Kelly and Ms. J.

Everyone began to cry. Ms. J stood up.

"Now, all this crying is not going to help. I really need your support and strength. You all are like family to us, and I know I can depend on you to help us through this time."

"Absolutely," cried Pat.

"Anything you need," added Belinda.

"Well, I do need a ride to chemo on Monday," said Ms. J.

"I'll take you," said Pat.

"I'll cook dinner," said Belinda.

Everyone looked shocked. Belinda didn't cook often, and when she did, it usually didn't turn out well.

"We'll make sure we stop to get some food on the way home," said Pat, laughing.

"Okay, I'll order some food. Is that better?" asked Belinda.

***

Charlie and Pat returned home, still upset about the news they heard.

"It's about time you got back. What was I supposed to do for dinner?" snapped Dan.

"Dan, not tonight. I just found out that Jeri has cancer, and I'm not in the mood for your foolishness."

"I don't care what she has. I'm hungry."

"Well dang it, Dan, go fix yourself something to eat because I'm not."

"Don't you raise your voice at me," shouted her husband. "You care more about that Afro coon than you care about me. I didn't know I married a nigger lover."

"Daddy you're so mean. I hate you," said Charlie as she ran upstairs.

"Dan, when did you get so mean and disgusting? Was it because Ms. Suzzette from up the street complained to the homeowners association because you basically turned our front yard into a soccer field? I didn't blame her. It looked awful. Because she was Black, does that mean you have issues with all Black people? Have you forgotten how much they helped us when you lost your job? Did you forget that Gerald got you the job you have now? How do you think the mortgage got paid? Yeah, Dan, Gerald gave me the money. I lied when I told you I got a bonus at work. Have you forgotten how Jeri always included Charlie in everything? How she paid for her to go to the overnight summer camp. How she made sure she got to practice before you became the coach? "I'm going to be there for Jeri and Kiersten. If you don't like it, well, you can just go to hell." Dan stood there in shock. His wife had never spoken to him like that before.

Chapter Six

Three months had passed, and Ms. J sat at her kitchen table, crying. She had lost her hair and some weight from the chemotherapy treatment. The doorbell rang, but she didn't answer. The door opened, and someone called out to her. It was Pat.

"Jeri," she called out again as she walked through the house. She walked into the kitchen. "Hey, Jeri, sorry to just drop by. I tried calling, but I think something is wrong with your phone.

Ms. J didn't reply but just sat, staring at a piece of paper that had "EVICTION NOTICE" written on it in large red letters.

"Jeri, what's going on?"

Ms. J pulled herself together to speak.

"My insurance isn't covering my treatments. I've been using our savings to pay for the treatments, and I haven't been able to pay my mortgage. I haven't been able to pay Kiersten's tuition. Now, we're going to have to move, and I'm going to have to take her out of her school. I have no idea where we're going to go. I haven't been able to work. I don't know what to do," she cried. "I can't even afford to take care of JJ."

Patricia hugged Ms. J. "This isn't your fault. You'll make it through all of this. You're, by far, the strongest person I know. You have the most amazing, understanding daughter."

"Her heart's going to be broken when I tell her she's going to have to change schools. She just got back into the swing of things there."

"She'll understand."

"I know, but her life is about to completely change again, and it's my fault. She's been so strong for me, but I know she's hurting not only for me but still from the car accident. I can't imagine what she's going through, but she's keeping a smile on her face for me. I hate that she's going through this alone."

"She has us, her friends, and her teachers. She's not alone."

"You all have been great. Her teacher, Mrs. Watkins, has been wonderful. She got her all caught up with her work. I'm surprised she's still teaching. She got her doctorate last year and said she was planning on being an administrator."

"I know, and she would not be happy if she finds out that I told you this, but she told me she decided to stay at the school another year specifically to be there for Kiersten, even though there was an opening for a principal at another school that she could easily have gotten."

"I can believe that; she's an amazing woman."

The doorbell rang. "I'll go see who's at the door," said Pat.

She opened the door to find her husband standing there, looking sheepish. "What are you doing here, Dan?"

"I know I'm the last person you want to see, but I miss you. I miss the kids too."

"Well, you should have thought about that when you were bullying everyone, and the fact that you didn't want me to be here for Jeri is absolutely unbelievable and cruel.

"I know, and I'm sorry. The last couple of months away from you, I realize now how terrible I was. I realize just how much I love you and our kids."

"We can talk about this later. I need to go back in to be with Jeri."

"Can I see her? I want to apologize. I want her to know that I know how good her family has been to us."

"Dan, I don't believe you. You haven't called or anything, yet you want me to think you've completely changed. "

"Just let me in so I can apologize to Jeri."

"I don't know if she wants to see anybody, especially you, so let me go ask her. Come in but just stay here until I go ask her."

Dan stepped into the house. Pat went into the kitchen to ask Jeri if she wanted to see Dan. Dan began snooping around the room. He started looking through Ms. J's mail. He took a couple pieces of mail and hid them in his pocket. Pat returned.

"She said she would see you," said Pat.

"You know, it's probably better that I don't see her," he said as he walked out the door.

"I knew you hadn't changed," shouted Pat. "You should be ashamed of yourself!"

Dan kept walking and didn't look back.

Pat walked back into the kitchen with Ms. J.

"Where's Dan?" asked Ms. J.

"He had to leave. I just don't get him. He wants me to think he's changed, but he leaves instead of apologizing like he said he would. I'm sorry he disturbed you.

"Believe it or not, for some reason, I think he has changed. It took a lot for him to come here," said Ms. J. "Maybe he just got cold feet."

"I really can't believe how we all miss him. The kids hear the voice messages he leaves, and we all wonder if he's sincere. We're all going out to dinner Friday, and I'll decide whether or not he'll be moving back home. Well, I don't want to keep talking about him. Let's focus on getting you better.

"Honestly, I'm afraid that I won't get better. Even if I were able to get in touch with Viv, I couldn't afford the treatment.

Pat looked very sad. "Jeri, I know you don't want to talk about this, but…" Pat hesitated. "You should reconsider filing a lawsuit against the driver of that truck and the company.

"I can't," replied Ms. J.

"I know you feel like you would be profiting from your family's death, but you wouldn't be. You'd be doing what you have to so you can be here for Kiersten. Just think about it, okay?"

CHap+ER SEVEn

Ms. J and Kiersten had to move to a tiny one-bedroom apartment in a low-income area. Ms. J could no longer pay for chemo, and after spending 2 months in the hospital, they had sent her home to be comfortable in her final days, lying in a hospital bed in the living room of their apartment. She had lost a lot of weight and looked frail. She hadn't been able to keep in touch with Pat or any of her friends because she couldn't pay their cell phone bill. But Kiersten still carried around her cell phone just to listen to Josie's message. Kiersten also had lost a lot of weight and still wore extremely short hair in solidarity with her mom. Kiersten, much like her mother, was very proud and didn't like to ask for help. She also didn't talk to adults about her situation because she was afraid they would take her away from her mom and put her in a foster home.

Early one Wednesday morning, Kiersten went into the living room to check on her mom and to give her some medicine.

"Good morning, Momma."

"Good morning, sweetie," said Ms. J softly.

"It's time to take your medicine." She raised her mom's bed up so she could drink.

"Baby, I need you to go to school today. You're in high school now, and missed days will not look good on your transcripts. You still want to go to Georgia Tech, right?"

"Yes, ma'am, but I need to be here for you. When I left you Friday, you hurt your arm."

"It was just a little slip. I'll be okay. But knowing that you're at school will make me feel better."

"I wish I could be homeschooled like I did for a few months last year."

"I know, baby. I'm sorry, but I can't afford wifi or a computer for you," Ms. J said with tears in her eyes.

"No, Mom, I didn't mean to make you feel bad. I just love you and want to be here to take care of you. Please don't cry. Okay, I'll go to school."

"Thank you, baby. How's school? Have you made new friends?"

"School is great. Yes, ma'am, I've made a lot of friends. I mean, none as cool as Kelly, Bella, and Abbie." She didn't want to tell her that everyone picked on her because she had short hair and made fun of her because she had to wear the same clothes all the time. She didn't tell her how, even though she was the smartest in her class, her teacher, Ms. Benton wouldn't let her represent the school in the math bowl because she said no baldheaded girl with wrinkle clothes should represent the school. She didn't tell her how Ms. Benton was trying to get her taken out of advanced classes, although she had all A's, how they picked on her when she was at school crying or the fact that she was caught sneaking her lunch home so she and Ms. J would have something to eat. She heard her technology teacher laughing, telling the other teachers that she caught her applying for food stamps on the computer at school. No one bothered to ask her what was going on or if she needed some help. She absolutely hated that school.

"I knew you'd be okay," said Ms. J.

Kiersten fought back her tears. "Yes, ma'am, I am."

"That's good, baby; that's good," said Ms. J as she closed her eyes.

Mom, I have everything set up for you right here. There's juice, crackers, and your medicine. Ms. Jackie from next door said she would check in on you, so I'm going to leave the door unlock. She's been very nice. She gave us the crackers and juice, although she really couldn't afford to."

Ms. Jackie was elderly and on her own. Kiersten had never seen anyone there to visit her, so she stopped in to see if she needed help. Kiersten would do chores for her and go to the store. She would pay Kiersten a couple of dollars when she could.

Ms. J had fallen asleep.

"I love you, Mom," said Kiersten as she kissed her mom on the check. She wiped the tears from her eyes and headed out the door. She checked her mailbox and got excited when she saw that her food stamp card arrived. She thought of the great dinner she would cook for her mom and Ms. Jackie when she got home from school.

Kiersten entered the school building with a smile on her face, which quickly turned to a frown when she saw the girls who were mean to her and picked on her for no reason.

"Hey, baldy," shouted one girl.

Another girl came up behind her and popped her on the head. "Girl, I have more hair on my knuckles than you do on your head, you bald-headed freak.

"Yeah, all you do is cry," said another girl. "You're a super freak.

Another girl grabbed her book bag and slung it across the hall. All her books and her phone came out of the bag.

"Look; super freak has a phone," said one girl.

"Who in the hell wants to talk to you," said another. The girl took Kiersten's phone and walked away.

"Give me my phone, Jadelyn," shouted Kiersten.

The girl ran down the hall and Kiersten chased her. Ms. Benton stopped Kiersten, although she saw the other girl running as well.

"Kiersten, you know that running is prohibited in the hallways."

"She took my phone."

"Well, you shouldn't have it at school," said Ms. Benton. "You're lucky we have a new principal today. If it weren't her first day, I would send you right up there to her. Now get to class.

Later that day, in Ms. Benton's class, Jadelyn taunted Kiersten about her phone. She pretended to make calls. Kiersten was getting upset. She raised her hand, but Ms. Benton ignored her.

"I need you all to work on your projects while I run to the media center. There should be no talking, and no one should get out of their seat."

As soon as Ms. Benton left the room, the girls started picking on Kiersten.

"Hey, cry baby, you want your phone back?" Jadelyn powered on the phone. "This phone doesn't even have service. I should've known you couldn't afford to have a phone." She slammed the phone on the floor.

"No!" shouted Kiersten. She got up to get her phone. Someone tripped her as she headed toward the phone. Jadelyn started stomping the phone to pieces. As Kiersten reached for the phone, Jadelyn stepped on her hand. Kiersten pushed Jadelyn from the phone. She was upset because Jadelyn had destroyed her phone and she would no longer have her voicemail from Josie. Ms. Benton entered the classroom just as Kiersten roughly pushed Jadelyn from her phone.

"That's it! You're going to the office," shouted Ms. Benton. Get your stuff and take this note I'm writing to the office. I hate that our new principal will have to deal with you on her first day. You, with your skinny body and raggedy clothes, do not represent the other students in this school."

Kiersten picked up her books and waited on Ms. Benton to finish the note. She fought back her tears because she didn't want to give them another reason to taunt her.

Kiersten sat in the office, waiting for the new principal to see her.

"Kiersten?" she heard a familiar voice question. She looked up to see Mrs. Watkins standing before her.

Mrs. Watkins, now Dr. Watkins, was the new principal. Kiersten couldn't believe she was seeing a familiar face.

"Come here, sweetheart," said Dr. Watkins as she stood in her office doorway.

Kiersten went to Dr. Watkins, who hugged her. Kiersten began to cry. She cried so hard. She let out all the tears that she had been holding back for the past three months. She held on tightly to Dr. Watkins, who tried to calm her down.

"Shh, it's okay, it's okay," said Dr. Watkins. Kiersten released her grip on Dr. Watkins. She escorted Kiersten into her office and closed the door.

"I didn't know you were a student here. We all were wondering where you were. I've stayed in touch with a lot of the parents and teachers and told them to contact me if they ever got in touch with you or your mom. I can't tell you how happy I am to see you."

Kiersten was still crying. "I'm happy to see you too. I can't believe you're here."

Dr. Watkins read the note Ms. Benton sent with Kiersten. "What's going on, Kiersten?" asked Dr. Watkins.

"Jadelyn broke my phone."

Dr. Watkins knew that Kiersten had that message from Josie on her phone.

"I told Ms. Benton that she took it, but Ms. Benton did nothing. Everyone in this school is just so mean.

"I'm sorry that you're having a hard time here. I know that you're a wonderful person and a great student. Trust me; I will take care of this." She handed Kiersten some tissues. Wipe your face, sweetie. It's going to be okay. How's your mom?"

"She's not doing so well. The doctors have given up on her. She's trying to stay strong for me. I don't know what I'll do if I lose her."

"So, you still haven't heard from your auntie?"

"No, ma'am. She couldn't get in touch with us now even if she wanted to. She doesn't have our address, and our phones are off.

"So you've been taking care of your mom and yourself."

"Yes, ma'am. Recently, our neighbor has helped some. She noticed that I would have to miss school to take care of my mom. She's elderly and kinda sick herself, so I help her out a lot. It's gotten pretty bad. I mean our neighbor barely has enough food for herself, but she still shares with us. I do errands for her, cook, and clean. She watches momma when I come to school. But I really don't like leaving my mom. I just feel that something will happen while I'm at school."

Dr. Watkins tried desperately to fight back her tears, but she couldn't. She stood and hugged Kiersten. "I'm here now. I'll talk to Mrs. Benton after school and come by your place this evening.

"I don't know if my mom will want you to see her like she is now," said Kiersten.

"I know your mom pretty well. While I know she's very proud; she's going to be happy to know that someone familiar is going to take care of you and help her as much as possible."

"Thank you, Ms…. I mean, Dr. Watkins," said Kiersten as she gave her a big hug.

"Go back to class. I'm actually going to visit your class to hear some of your projects later today. How's that going for you?"

"I'm finished with mine. Well, after what's just happened, I need to add another slide. But I'll be ready by the time you come."

Kiersten went back to class, feeling much better but still upset about her phone. Dr. Watkins found Pat McLendon's number and called her. She got her home voicemail.

"Hi, Mrs. McLendon, this is Vanessa Watkins. I have some unbelievable news. I have found our girl. Kiersten is going to Washington High School, where I just became the principal. I have her address; it's 1315 Brokpo Lane in Langston. It sounds like Mrs. J isn't doing so well. It would be great if you could get by there to see her. Kiersten said her neighbor looks in on her mom so her door is probably unlocked and you can just go in.

Mr. McLendon stood by the machine, listening. He deleted the message, got in his truck, and headed over to Ms. J's apartment. He sat outside her apartment as if he were contemplating going inside. Finally, he grabbed some papers out of his glove compartment and went into the apartment.

Ms. Jackie saw him go into the apartment. She was worried because she had never seen him before or anyone else at the apartment. In spite of her fears, she gathered herself to go check on Ms. J. It took a few minutes. She grabbed her cane and went into the apartment.

"Who are you," she asked.

"I'm a friend."

"Well, why haven't I seen you before, and what's that you're having her signing? She's ain't in no shape to be signing anything."

Mr. McLendon quickly grabbed the papers and ran down the stairs to his car.

"Honey, you alright?" she asked Ms. J.

Ms. J had fallen back asleep. Ms. Jackie decided to stay with Ms. J until Kiersten came home from school.

***

It was the final period of the day, and, as promised, Dr. Watkins visited Ms. Benton's class to hear some presentations.

"Okay, who wants to go first?" Ms. Benton asked. Tamiya and Kiersten were the only students to raise their hands. "Okay, Tamiya, you can go ahead." Tamiya presented her project, and the class applauded.

"Alright, who wants to go next?" Kiersten and Mauricio were the only students with their hands up. "Mauricio, I would choose you, but I'm sure Dr. Watkins wants to hear someone who can clearly speak English." She chuckled and looked at Dr. Watkins, who wasn't smiling.

"Tiana, what about you? Are you ready to present?" asked Ms. Benton.

"Um, did I have my hand raised?" replied Tiana.

"Kiersten, go ahead with your presentation," said Dr. Watkins.

Kiersten stood to walk to the front of the room. One of the girls stuck her foot out to trip her. She didn't fall. She was on a mission.

"My project is titled What a Difference a Year Makes."

She went to her next slide. "This is a picture of my family on my 13th birthday just a year ago. That's my mom, who everyone calls Ms. J; my dad, who everyone calls Mr. G; my beautiful little sister Josie; and my handsome brother Justin. That's my then-pregnant Aunt Viv and Uncle Fred who surprised me by coming all the way from California to be here for my birthday. That cute little puppy there was my birthday present. I named him JJ after my sister and brother.

As you can see from everyone's big smiles, it was a great time. The class gasped to see Kiersten with beautiful long hair and nice clothes. "In the background, you can see our indoor pool."

The class was shocked. The next slide was a collage of her friends and of her house. "These are my best friends, and that cute boy was my first boyfriend."

All the students were looking at each other with disbelief. Kiersten went to the next slide.

"This is a picture of my dad, brother, sister, and uncle leaving to go to the store that night."

The next slide was of a badly wrecked SUV.

"This is a picture of my dad's SUV after being hit by a semi-truck." Notice the yellow tape around the vehicle. That's because the accident took the lives of my dad, sister, brother, and uncle."

The class and Ms. Benton were shocked and saddened.

"The next picture is a selfie of me in the mirror with my phone. Until today, that phone didn't leave my side because I would listen to the message my sister managed to leave me right before she died in the accident. It was the last time she told me she loved me."

Jadelyn put her head down in shame.

"This next picture is of me getting my head shaved to show support for my mom, who found out she had cancer three months after our family was killed."

"This is a picture of us moving out of our house. We had to move because my mom's insurance wouldn't pay for my mom's treatments, and she had to use all of her savings to pay her doctor bills. The other picture is me giving my dog to my neighbor because we could no longer afford to take care of him."

The next picture was a picture of Ms. J in her hospital bed in her living room. "This is a picture of my mom fighting for her life."

"This is a picture of me staying home from school to take care of my mom."

"The last photo is of my neighbor and me praying. I pray that, somehow, I can get in touch with my mom's twin sister, my Aunt Viv, who I know would be a bone marrow match for my mom. I pray that, somehow, we'll be able to afford the treatments my mom needs. I pray that the kids in this school would leave me alone. I pray that the teachers here would treat me fairly, regardless of how I look. And, to be honest, I pray for food."

The entire class was crying or had tears in their eyes.

"I wanted to have one more slide. It would have been of me smiling when I saw Dr. Watkins today. Dr. Watkins was my teacher and mentor at my previous school. Like she has always done, she actually gave me hope that things will be okay. I haven't been this happy in over a year."

Dr. Watkins walked to the front of the class.

"Dr. Watkins, about that note I sent with Kiersten—" began Ms. Benton.

Dr. Watkins cut her off. "We'll talk about that after class."

Dr. Watkins addressed the class. "I hope you all have learned a lesson from Kiersten's project. It's never okay to mistreat someone. You never know what that person might be going through. Kiersten has had to struggle to take care of her mom, help her elderly neighbor, and maintain her A average. Coming to school should not be an added stress for her. She's dealing with the loss of her family and the fact that she can't get in touch with her aunt, and you decide because she has short hair, you're going to make fun of her. Not one of you tried to be a friend to her or ask her what was going on, my staff included. I'm very ashamed and disappointed. I had no idea that I was coming into a school where so many of the students and faculty were bullies.

Jadelyn raised her hand. "Yes?" asked Dr. Watkins.

Jadelyn stood up, crying. "I just want to apologize to Kiersten." She turned to Kiersten. "I'm so sorry for destroying your phone. I'm sorry for being so mean to you. I've treated you like crap for no reason. I have the same phone as yours, and you can have my phone. All you have to do is put your SIM card in my phone, and you'll have your sister's voicemail back."

Everyone started apologizing to Kiersten. Mauricio stood up. "Sit down—" started Ms. Benton until she saw the look on Dr. Watkins face.

"Go ahead, Mauricio," said Dr. Watkins.

"I just wanna tell Kiersten I'm sorry I no stand up for her. I also wanna donate all the money I got. It not much but I think if everyone donate, it will make a difference."

"I don't have money, but I'll donate my time to come help you do chores," said another student.

"I think we should start a Go Fund Me page," said Aiden, another student.

The bell rang, and everyone came up to Kiersten, hugging her and wishing her well. Some said they would pray for her and her mom.

"Stay strong, sista," said another student.

Dr. Watkins stayed after class to talk to Ms. Benton.

"Ms. Benton, the way you talked about Kiersten in this note, is terrible. I can't believe you would say the things you said and think it would be okay. What does Kiersten having short hair or, as you refer to her as this baldheaded child, have to do with her behavior. I have read your file, and there are several complaints about you mistreating students, and leaving your class alone without adult supervision earlier today was inexcusable. You obviously aren't happy here, so we're going to make this your last day.

Chapter Eight

Kiersten couldn't wait to get home to tell her mom about Dr. Watkins. Ms. J was sleeping. Kiersten heard a knocking on the wall. That meant Ms. Jackie next door needed her, so she went next door. She knocked on the screen door, as the main door was already open.

"Come on in," said Ms. Jackie. "Baby, do your mama have some White friends?"

"Yes, ma'am, but we haven't seen them since we moved here. They don't know where we live."

"Well, there was a White man in your apartment today."

Kiersten got scared. "There shouldn't have been a White man or any man in our apartment."

"I think he made your mama sign something."

"Oh no, I need to call the police."

Kiersten used Ms. Jackie's phone to call the police and waited for two hours, but they didn't come. She had to leave to walk to the store before it got dark. She let Ms. Jackie know that she was going to store and that she would be making spaghetti. She also let her know that Dr. Watkins would be stopping by.

"Hi, Kiersten," said Mr. Ravi, the store owner, when she arrived at the store.

"Hi, Mr. Ravi," said Kiersten with a smile.

"Kiersten! You're smiling. You have good news?"

"Yes, sir. I did everything you told me to do. Look; I got a food stamp card. Now I can cook my mom some real food. I know she's tired of the soup."

"You have to be careful. She won't be able to eat anything too heavy."

"I know; I'm making spaghetti. I'm going to use a light sauce with some toast. I'm getting ginger ale too. That's her favorite soda."

"I'm so happy it worked out for you."

"That's not all. My favorite teacher from my old school is my new principal.

Not only that but I finally talked about my family's accident and my mom's illness in front of my class. It was really hard for me to tell everyone what happened and I was so afraid I'd break down and cry, but, you know, it made me feel good. The bullies in the class apologized. I'm actually looking forward to going to school tomorrow. But I got some scary news when I got home. My neighbor told me a man was in our apartment. I called the police, but no one came."

"Did you ask your mom about the man?"

"I tried, but she was sleeping."

"Hold on," said Mr. Ravi. He picked up the phone and called the police. A couple of minutes later, two policemen were at the store.

"What's going on?" asked the police. "Did you catch her stealing? I swear; you people are always stealing."

"Don't jump to conclusions," said the other policeman.

"This is Kiersten Shorter," said Mr. Ravi angrily to the cop who jumped to conclusions.

"Kiersten Shorter?" asked the other police-man.

"Yes," replied Mr. Ravi. The policeman stared at Kiersten for a minute.

"Is your mom's name Jeri?"

"You know this criminal?" asked the first officer.

"Doug, I told you not to jump to conclusions. I got this; just go wait in the car."

"How do you know my mom?"

"I really don't know your mom, but your uncle saved my life. Actually, your brother and sister asking him to help me was what saved me. Your dad kept your uncle calm enough so he would want to help me. I was choking. Your family were heroes."

Kiersten was proud to hear that news.

"So what's going on?" asked Officer Kilpatrick.

"My neighbor said there was a man in our apartment today. There shouldn't been a man in our apartment."

"What do you mean apartment? Don't you live in Sweetwater subdivision?" asked Officer Kilpatrick.

"No, sir, we had to move," replied Kiersten. "My neighbor got a good look at the man. Can you please talk to her?

"I sure will. Come on; it's getting dark. I'll give you a ride home."

"I have to finish getting some items so I can cook tonight," replied Kiersten.

"Go ahead and take your time," said the officer.

While Kiersten shopped for her items, two Black male teenagers walked into the store.

"Officer Pete," said one of the teens as he gave the officer a high five.

"You young men just coming from basketball practice?"

"Yeah, and you know I was crossing them up," said the teen.

"I tried that old timer rocker step you showed me, and it actually worked," teased one of the teens.

"Don't hate on the old school," said the officer as he laughed. In the last year since Kiersten's family saved his life, Officer Pete had changed his views about people. He had decided to treat all people equally.

Kiersten found all the ingredients she needed to make the best spaghetti. She put everything on the counter.

"Looks like you're going to make some good spaghetti tonight," said Mr. Ravi. "I'm sure she's going to be very happy. Here, give her this rose. Tell her I hope she feels better soon, and I look forward to seeing her.

Mr. Ravi saw the confusion on Officer Pete's face.

"I pray that she beats this cancer," he added.

Cancer, thought, Officer Pete. *This poor child has been going through hell.*

Mr. Ravi packed Kiersten's bag, and Officer Pete took them to his car.

"So, we're a taxi service now?" complained Officer Pete's partner.

"Shut up, Doug," said Officer Pete. "We're going to investigate a possible 10-22."

"The only suspicious person I see is sitting in the back seat."

"I said, shut up."

They arrived at Kiersten's apartment. Dr. Watkins was sitting by Ms. J's side.

"It's about time," said Dr. Watkins to Officer Pete. "Ms. Jackie next door told me Kiersten called you almost three hours ago."

"Dr. Watkins, this is Officer Kilpatrick—" began Kiersten.

"Officer Pete," he interrupted. "Nice to meet you."

"My Uncle Fred saved his life."

Dr. Watkins was confused. Officer Pete explained while Kiersten took the groceries into her tiny kitchen.

Officer Pete went next door to get a description of the man who was at the apartment. He returned and told Kiersten that he had the description and that he would keep an eye on her apartment. He also suggested that she not leave the door unlocked.

"I'm taking her to get a duplicate key made for Ms. Jackie tonight," said Dr. Watkins.

***

Later that evening, Ms. J was awake and had finished eating. Dr. Watkins was still there. Ms. J was in good spirits, unlike she had been for months. Knowing that Dr. Watkins was there to help make her feel better. They didn't mention the man who came into the apartment because they didn't want to upset her.

Chapter Nine

The next morning, Kiersten was awakened by Ms. Jackie beating on the wall. Kiersten took a few minutes to gather herself and checked on her mom. She opened the door and saw a gift bag in front of her door. She looked in the bag and found a new school outfit. She entered Ms. Jackie's apartment to thank her for the gift.

"Sugar, I wish I could've bought you an outfit, but I didn't buy it.

"Dr. Watkins must have bought it," said Kiersten

"I don't know who bought it, but I was knocking because that man was back. I think I scared him away when I started yelling."

Kiersten got scared. "Officer Pete said he would come by this morning before I leave for school. I'm going to stay home until he comes."

"I'm going to sit with your mama. You go to school. I'm going to bring old Hammerin' Hank with me," she said as she picked up her baseball bat. "Baby, do you know who Hank Aaron is?"

Kiersten thought, *of course, I do*. You've only *told me how you saw him hit his 755th home run on July 20th, 1976 about 755 times*. "Yes, ma'am, he played for the Atlanta Braves." She thought that by saying yes this time, she wouldn't get the full story. She was wrong.

As promised, Officer Pete came by. She told him that the man had come back to the apartment.

"You go to school," said Officer Pete. We'll take care of your mom.

Kiersten couldn't believe that she was looking forward to school. She had on the new outfit that Dr. Watkins bought her, and she knew she wouldn't be bullied.

She stopped by Dr. Watkins's office to thank her for the outfit.

"I love the outfit, but I didn't buy it," said Dr. Watkins.

"Really?" questioned Kiersten. "Someone left it at my door.

***

At the McLendon house, Dan was working on his laptop while Pat sat watching the news. Dan got a text message.

"Pat, come ride with me somewhere," said Mr. McLendon.

"Where are you going?" asked Ms. McLendon.

"Just trust me; come on," replied Mr. McLendon.

Ms. McLendon got in the car and saw an envelope addressed to Ms. J.

"Why do you have this letter?" asked Ms. McLendon.

"Trust me," said Mr. McLendon.

***

Back at Kiersten's school, kids gave their presentation. They had a substitute teacher named Mrs. Davis. Dr. Watkins came to the door with a big smile.

"Excuse me, Mrs. Davis, but can I borrow Kiersten for a moment? Actually, you stay right there, Kiersten.

"Hey, Dr. Watkins," shouted a student. "We started a Go Fund Me for Kiersten's mom last night, and it already has over $25,000."

"Wow," said Dr. Watkins. "You see; a little compassion goes a long way. Since you know what's going on with Kiersten, I'm going to let you in on this surprise."

Kiersten sat in anticipation. In came Ms. Pat. Kiersten was so excited to see Ms. Pat that she quickly got up and hugged her. The class sat and watched Kiersten's excitement. They had no idea who Ms. Pat was but figured she had to be some-one special.

"I'm so happy to see you, Ms. Pat."

"I'm happy to see you, too. I had no idea where you were. We have a big surprise for you."

"I thought you were my surprise," said Kiersten.

In walked the biggest surprise.

"Aunt Viv!" shouted Kiersten. They embraced. "Aunt Viv, Aunt Viv," said Kiersten repeatedly. There wasn't a dry eye in the classroom. Kiersten couldn't stop crying. She was excited to see Aunt Viv. She knew she was there to save her mom's life. After a few minutes, Kiersten was able to calm down. "I can't believe it's you; where's Fredricka?"

"It's me, baby girl," cried Aunt Viv. "Sweetie, believe me; if I had known Jeri needed me, I would've been here months ago. I'm so sorry, baby. I left Fredricka with her grandparents in California. I'll go get her once we get Jeri better."

"I know you would've been here," cried Kiersten. "I'm so glad Dr. Watkins was able to get in touch with you."

"Dr. Watkins didn't get in touch with me, sweetie," replied Aunt Viv.

"Thank you for finding her," Kiersten said to Ms. Pat.

"It wasn't me. It was actually Coach McLendon," said Ms. Pat.

"Coach? Where is he?" asked Kiersten.

"He's in the car," said Ms. Pat. He hired a private investigator, and when Dr. Watkins called yesterday to let us know she found you, he contacted her and she was on the first plane here this morning.

"Coach McLendon did that for me?"

"He did it for all of us. We all want your mom to get better," said Ms. Pat as she pulled out an envelope from her purse. "Look what else he did," said Ms. Pat. She handed the envelope to Kiersten and told her to open it. Kiersten was still hugging Aunt Viv and didn't want to let her go.

"Go ahead, baby, open it. I'm not going anywhere," said Aunt Viv.

Kiersten pulled out a check for 47 million dollars made payable to her mom. Kiersten stared at the check in disbelief.

"Yes, honey, your mom and I talked about su-ing the truck driver and his company who hit your dad. At first, she was against the idea, but in our last conversation, she said she would do anything to be around for you. You guys moved away before we could do anything. I mentioned this to Dan in passing and, without my knowing, he sued the company. He had to get power of attorney over your mom to get the check. I believe he went by your apartment to have your mom sign over power of attorney.

"So, he's the person that my neighbor saw. I bet he left this outfit too."

"Yes, he did," said Ms. Pat. "He had a little help picking it out, too. Girls!" called Ms. Pat. In walked Kelly, Abbie, Bella, and Charlie. Kiersten was speechless and stood shocked. Eventually, Kiersten ran to her best friends, and they circled around her for a group hug. Kiersten tried to speak but she couldn't from all the tears. Kelly, Abbie, Bella, and Charlie just held her tighter. Kiersten stood up straight and wiped her face with her sleeves. "I've missed y'all so much," Kiersten said with a knot in her throat.

"We've missed you too!" Bella said.

"Yeah, we talked about you every day," Abbie said, still wiping tears from her face.

"Good! For a second, I thought y'all forgot about me," Kiersten said.

"We could never forget about you. You're like the glue to the puzzle that keeps us together," said Abbie. They confusedly looked at Abbie. "What?" Abbie asked.

"Abbie, you don't use glue for puzzles," Kiersten said, laughing.

"Ugh, y'all know I'm not good at this analogy stuff," said Abbie, laughing.

"What she's trying to say is that everything felt empty without you and we missed you a lot," said Kelly.

That evening, they all went to visit Ms. J, who was asleep when they got there. They all sat around her telling stories about the past. Aunt Viv was lying in bed with her. She couldn't stop crying.

"Mommy," Kiersten said quietly. She didn't want to scare her. Ms. J opened her eyes. Everyone stood up. She saw a bunch of smiling faces starring at her.

"Am I dreaming?" she softly asked

"No, you're not," she heard a familiar voice softly say from behind her.

Ms. J turned her head, and, when she saw Aunt Viv, her face lit up with the biggest smile. Then she started crying.

"I'm so sorry I haven't been here for you," cried Aunt Viv. Ms. J patted Aunt Viv's arm that was around her.

All the girls wanted to hug Ms. J, but Ms. Pat said that is wasn't a good idea because of germs she might catch since her immune system was so weak.

"Where," Ms. J struggled to get her question out, "is Dan?" Although she was sick, she knew that Dan had fought to get her a settlement. She had no idea that he had also found Viv.

"He's in the car," replied Pat. "He was afraid that you wouldn't want him to come in.

"I do," said Ms. J.

"I'll go get him," said Ms. Pat.

Mrs. McLendon went outside the door and yelled down to Dan. She waved to him to come into the apartment then she went back in. A couple of minutes later, Dan came into the apartment. All of a sudden, the door flew open. It was Ms. Jackie wielding her bat.

"That's him, that's him," she yelled as she held her bat in the air.

"Ms. Jackie!" yelled Kiersten. "We know him, we know him."

"Well, who is he?" she asked.

Kiersten put her arm around him and said, "He's my Uncle Dan, and he's my hero."

***

Fifteen months later, Ms. J was fully recovered. She and Kiersten had settled into their new home, which was close to their old subdivision. She and Aunt Viv were preparing what looked like a feast.

"I've been looking forward to cooking this dinner for the last year," said Ms. J. "I want everyone to know how much their love and support meant to me."

"Jeri, you built a guest house for Ms. Jackie. I'm sure she knows," joked Aunt Viv.

Kiersten was setting the table with name cards. Little Fredricka followed, mixing them up. There was one for Mrs. & Mr. McLendon, Dr. Watkins, Mr. Ravi, and Ms. Jackie, among others.

Ding Dong!

"Kier, will you get the door, please?" asked Mrs. J with a big smile.

"Yes, ma'am," replied Kiersten.

Kiersten, assuming it was one of the dinner guests, opened the door without looking through the peephole. When she opened it, she didn't see anyone. She looked down and saw a fluffy white dog.

"JJ!" she shouted. JJ leaped into her arms.

THE END

ABOUt tHE AUtHOR

Brooklyn Wright is an honor student from Atlanta, Georgia. Brooklyn has a passion for community service and the betterment of the community; which, is evident in her first award-winning story-book, "The Adventures of Earth Saver Girl; Don't be a Litterbug." Besides reading and writing, Brooklyn loves playing sports and tutoring kids.

For more information about Brooklyn, visit her websites; www.brooklynwright.com and www.earthsavergirl.com.